Piece By Piece

Written by
Stephanie Shaw

Illustrated by
Sylvie Daigneault

To my sister, Kathleen Isabel, with gratitude and love.

—Stephanie

In memory of my mother, Lise, a skilled and creative seamstress.

—Sylvie

Sleeping Bear Press™
2395 South Huron Parkway, Suite 200
Ann Arbor, MI 48104
www.sleepingbearpress.com

Printed and bound in the United States.

10 9 8 7 6 5 4 3 2 1

Library of Congress Cataloging-in-Publication Data

Names: Shaw, Stephanie, author. | Daigneault, Sylvie, illustrator.
Title: Piece by piece / written by Stephanie Shaw ; illustrated by Sylvie Daigneault.
Description: Ann Arbor, MI : Sleeping Bear Press, [2017] | Summary: A weaver
dreams of being able to buy things for her children as she crafts a dress of dragon
scales and candle glow.
Identifiers: LCCN 2017002843 | ISBN 9781585369997 (hard cover)
Subjects: | CYAC: Weaving–Fiction. | Mother and child–Fiction.
Classification: LCC PZ7.S53434 Pie 2017 | DDC [E]–dc23
LC record available at https://lccn.loc.gov/2017002843

Once upon a time a weaver tucked a memory into her collection basket. All day she gathered them up: the crunch of leaves, the springiness of moss, the leap and splash of a fish.

At night she wove the day's bounty into cloth. It was rich. Exquisite. Unique.

"Tell us," asked her children. "Tell us where this came from."

The weaver held a piece of fabric to her nose. "Ah." She smiled. "The sweetness of a puppy!"

"What else?"

"The breath of a hot air balloon as it floats against a morning sky, and the squish of mud between your toes."

The weaver began to sew piece by piece.

Every now and then the children playing among the bolts of cloth asked, "Tell us about this one!"

And, of course, she did.

When the garment was finished, she laid it in a box.
The bodice was a sparkle of starlight with the skirt full
as a spring meadow. Along the edge was lace like the
foam of an ocean wave. Tucked in the folds of the gown
were treasures: some dragon scales, a pirate's sash, and
the red flash of a blackbird's wing.

The weaver closed her eyes. She dreamed of all she
could buy for her children with the money the dress
would bring: shoes of soft leather, loaves of thickly
braided bread, sweet crisp apples, and paper bags of
warm roasted nuts.

In the village the next day, she held the dress against her so a shopkeeper could see it.

"What's this?" the shopkeeper asked, pointing to the shimmering top.

"Starlight and candle glow."

"I could never sell this," he replied. "What absolute nonsense. I suggest you remove that part."

So the weaver returned home. She gently snipped at the threads that held the garment together.

Piece by piece, pale and shimmering cloth fell to the floor.

When the weaver returned to the shop, the shopkeeper frowned.

"Hmmm. What's all this?" he asked, pointing to the skirt held before him.

"A day when gentle breezes sway the tall grass and wildflowers," she answered.

"Oh, that's much too full! Much too much!" the shopkeeper's wife chimed in. "And what about that flounce at the edge?"

"The kiss of the sea as it reaches the shore."

"Well, we can't have any kissing!" said the shopkeeper. "That needs to go."

So the weaver returned home again.

The children watched as piece by piece an indigo night fell to the floor. The coo of a dove. The juiciness of a tangerine. A bit of coral from a tropical reef. The glint of a saber. The scent of chocolate and cinnamon.

"I've done as he asked," the weaver said to herself. She slowly walked to the shop.

The children ran ahead to the village fair, carrying a mysterious package.

"Now what have you brought us?" The shopkeeper peered over his glasses. His wife scowled.

"The wishes from a dandelion on a summer's day," said the weaver. "The whisper of fog rising from a lake. Frost caught on a spider's web."

He held the gauzy fabric up to the light.

"Bah!" he replied. "Too small! Too flimsy! No one has any use for this."

But the weaver turned away and used it to catch her tears.

As she left the shop, the children ran to her.
"Come and see what we made!"

At the village fair there were displays of golden honey, bunches of lavender, and pyramids of brilliant fruits and vegetables. Through row after row and stall after stall the children ran, pulling the weaver along.

Finally they came to where a crowd of people
gathered around a quilt hanging between two trees.

"Rich," said a woman.

"Exquisite," said another.

"Unique," said a third.

The shopkeeper, hearing the cheers from the square, pushed through the crowd. He did not bother to look at the quilt. His greedy eyes were on the people asking where they might buy something so beautiful for themselves.

He turned to the weaver and said, "You must sell this to me! And as many more as you can weave. We'll make a fortune selling them from my shop."

The weaver touched each piece of the quilt. The blueness of a robin's egg. A meringue of sky. She was sure she caught sight of a dragon's scale.

"Never," she whispered.

That night the weaver smoothed the new quilt as she tucked the children into bed.

"Tell us," they said.

The weaver moved her hand slowly across the pieces. She stopped when she came to one as soft as a pony's nose.

"Once upon a time," she said.

Author's Note

Patchwork quilts began when people could not afford to throw things away once they wore out. Scraps of old blankets, clothing, and feed sacks were used to patch blankets. At first, these were not fancy, but over time, making intricate patterns and designs from pieces of cloth became an art form. Today, many quilters carry on the tradition of creating beautiful blankets with pieces of fabric. Quilts can represent things such as a special occasion, a friendship, a place, or even the history of a country or family. In a way, they are "stories" told through the artwork of small pieces of material sewn together.

Writing a story is very much like creating a quilt. Writers collect ideas, memories, and word lists. These are the "scraps" that are pulled together and will form complete stories. Here are some ideas you can use to show a story through artwork:

Retell a story you have just read—only use pictures instead of words. Make drawings on equal-size pieces of paper or fabric that represent different characters and action from the story. Perhaps even try choosing colors that remind you of the tone or mood of the story. The squares can be detailed or symbols. Lay them out to design a "story quilt." [CCSS.ELA-LITERACY.CCRA.R4]*

You can also make a story quilt as a journal of a special event or even a whole school year. Each square tells only a *part* of the story but altogether you can show what happened over time. You can make a story quilt by yourself, with a partner, or with a whole classroom. [CCSS.ELA-LITERACY.CCRA.R.7]**

You might ask an older family member to tell you about something that happened before you were born. Perhaps you might look at photographs with them. Listen carefully. Then draw your own pictures to show what happened. [CCSS.ELA-LITERACY.CCRA.SL.1]*** and [CCSS.ELA-LITERACY.CCRA.SL.2]****

By using what you remember from the story (plus your own imagination), *piece by piece* you will create something rich, exquisite, and unique. Happy quilting!

FOR EDUCATORS

For easy incorporation into your classroom Language Arts units, we have noted a few of the relevant CCSS standards that can be used with this book.

* CCSS.ELA-LITERACY.CCRA.R.4
Interpret words and phrases as they are used in a text, including determining technical, connotative, and figurative meanings, and analyze how specific word choices shape meaning or tone.

** CCSS.ELA-LITERACY.CCRA.R.7
Integrate and evaluate content presented in diverse media and formats, including visually and quantitatively, as well as in words.

*** CCSS.ELA-LITERACY.CCRA.SL.1
Prepare for and participate effectively in a range of conversations and collaborations with diverse partners, building on others' ideas and expressing their own clearly and persuasively.

**** CCSS.ELA-LITERACY.CCRA.SL.2
Integrate and evaluate information presented in diverse media and formats, including visually, quantitatively, and orally.